THE

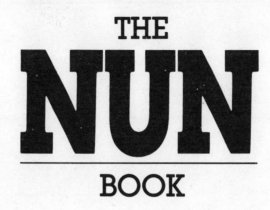

BOOK

Turnbull & Willoughby
Publishers

THE
NUN
BOOK

Bea Bourgeois
Tom Carey
Illustrated by Tom Olcese

First printing May 1986

10   9   8   7   6   5   4   3   2   1

Manufactured in the United States of America

ISBN: 0-943084-36-9

Published by Turnbull & Willoughby Publishers, Inc.
1151 West Webster, Chicago, IL 60614

I've Always Wanted to Know:

Ask and Ye Shall be Answered

Standard Nun (Antique Version)

Highly starched wimple; pleats ironed by novices in convent laundry

Habit — black, dark blue or brown, made of gabardine, wool or serge — Wt. approx. 12.5 lbs.

The Scapular of St. Dominic

Rosary made by retired nuns in infirmary

Sensible black Oxfords, Cuban heels

No hair

Plain wire rim frames

Highly starched collar (causes prickly heat in summer)

No discernible bosom

Key ring: Convent recreation room, church sanctuary, altar bread supply cabinet

Not shown — black Lisle stockings, round elastic garter above knee

Standard Nun (Contemporary Version)

Diane Von Furstenberg designer frames

Discernible bosom

Key ring: Convent's Ford Escort wagon, Kryptonite lock for 10-speed Gitane bike, Bingo supply cabinet

Sensible black Oxfords, Cuban heels

Hair — or, for older nuns, wig from World O'Wigs in neutral shade

Polyester print blouse — large floral motif in pinks and lime green

Polyester pantsuit

Not shown — knee-hi nylons

The Compleat Nun

Standard Operating Equipment

* rosary: small, medium, large, or extra-large: attached to belt of habit and draped gracefully along left hip

* several thousand boxes of colored stars, smiling jack-o-lanterns, snowmen, Easter bunnies, witches, hearts, and/or smiley faces to be pasted on top of spelling tests graded 100%

* one large metal clicker in the shape of a beetle, for use in keeping order as class files into church or forms any one of an endless number of two-by-two ranks to march somewhere

* lifetime supply of holy cards, to be awarded for polite behavior, academic achievement, or as encouragement for the student to consider a vocation to the convent or seminary

* slender wooden blackboard pointer with metal tip for showing the class where early missionaries were martyred; also effective as shoulder-tapping weapon or knuckle-rapper

* certificate showing completion of The Nun's Handwriting Course, perfectly written in Palmer Method letters

* spiritual reading, including such amusing tales as Butler's <u>Lives of the Saints</u> or <u>St. John of the Cross</u>, <u>Mystic and Martyr</u>, to be enjoyed during the 7 to 8 p.m. Recreation Hour after Sister finishes mending her stockings and cross-stitching an altar cloth

A Peek at the Sanctum Sanctorum

1   Narrow cot with metal frame — institutional type; crucifix on pillow

2   Straight back chair

3   Crucifix hanging on wall with palms blessed on Palm Sunday behind it

4   Photo on dresser — Sister and her parents on the day she was professed

5   Nightstand with bottle of holy water, rosary, prayer book

6   Holy water font underneath light switch shaped like an angel

7   Bedroom slippers — ugly old lady slippers on floor under nightstand

8   Sensible shoes, one pair

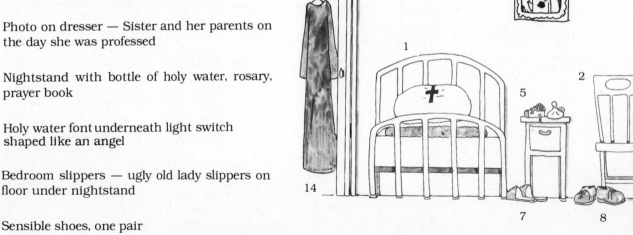

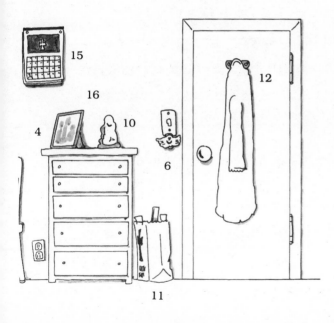

9 Picture of the Sacred Heart hanging on the wall

10 Statue of Infant of Prague on dresser

11 Shopping bag in corner loaded with free samples from Catholic School Teachers Convention — pencils, rulers, scratch pads

12 Flannel nightgown hanging on hook behind door

13 Afghan neatly folded at foot of bed; she crocheted it herself during Recreation

14 Habit hanging in closet, starched collar on closet shelf

15 Catholic calendar hanging on the wall, printed courtesy of the funeral home across the street from the church

16 No mirror on wall above dresser, to discourage sins of pride and self-respect

Parochial Profile

Sister Mary St. Sepulchre

HOME: The Convent of the Holy Shroud. Originally from Des Moines.

AGE: Can't remember. Thinks she entered the convent around 1931 or so.

PROFESSION: Bride of Christ. Also Lunchroom Spy, Spelldown Referee, Playground Monitor.

WHY I DO WHAT I DO: "To save my immortal soul and to be happy in Heaven with Jesus forever and ever."

QUOTE: "I before E, except after C, or when sounded like A, as in 'neighbor' and 'weigh.'"

FAVORITE MOVIE: "The Bells of St. Mary's."

HOBBY: Crocheting Kleenex box covers to sell at the Holy Shroud Fun Festival. "This is God's work on earth."

FAVORITE SCOTCH: None

A Day In The Life Of Sister Mary St. Sepulchre

5:30 a.m. Three rings on the loud, shrill convent bell. Sister thanks God for a new day. Sister wishes she could sleep till noon. Sister says, "Praise be the name of Jesus" and heads for the community bathroom.

5:32 a.m. Personal hygiene.

5:45 a.m. Sister dons the habit and says a little prayer for the nun who invented starched collars and cuffs, six layers of wool and gabardine, veils, wimples, coifs, and round headed pins to keep it all together.

6:15 a.m. Morning Offering. Make bed. Dust Infant of Prague statue. Straighten picture of Blessed Frances Cabrini. Hide copy of The Thorn Birds under nightgown in bottom dresser drawer.

6:30 a.m. Mass. Pray for guidance. Pray for forgiveness. Pray for a blizzard.

7:00 a.m. Breakfast in convent refectory. Stewed prunes, one soft-cooked egg, skim milk, 100% Bran Flakes, wheat toast.

7:30 a.m. Unlock classroom. Write on blackboard, "Good Morning, Children. Jesus Loves You."

8:00 a.m. to 3:00 p.m. Follow lesson plans for Religion, Spelling, Reading, Science, Music, Art, Geography, History, Social Studies, Penmanship. Take attendance. Send milk money to the office. Collect permission slips for field trip to the Natural Wonder Pumpkin Farm. Play "Red Rover" during Recess. Take two aspirin with lunch.

6:00 p.m. Dinner in convent refectory. Tuna-noodle casserole, cottage cheese with canned peach slices, rye bread, Postum.

7:00 p.m.
to
8:00 p.m. Recreation. Darn stockings, find three pieces in community jigsaw puzzle, read Chapter V in <u>Father Damien: Friend of the Lepers.</u>

8:30 p.m. Chapel. Evening prayers. Examine conscience. Think about asking Mother Superior for a year's sabbatical.

Application to the Postulancy
Sorrowful Sisters of St. Symphorosa

Name: Mary Eileen O'Dowd Cabrini de Nepomuc

Address: 123 Ora Pro Nobis Drive, Centerville

Grade School: Mystical Martyrdom

High School: Stabat Mater Dolorosa Academy

Height: 4' 11" Weight: 164 Birth Date: 4/19/70

Hobbies: I just love to feed the hungry, shelter the homeless, give drink to the thirsty, clothe the naked, visit the imprisoned, visit the sick, and bury the dead. I also crochet and play the accordion.

Why Do You Want To Become A Sorrowful Sister: To know, love, and serve God in this world and to be happy with Him forever in Heaven. I also look good in black, and I have lovely handwriting.

Who Are Your Favorite Saints: I have always loved dear St. Symphorosa, whose seven sons were all martyred under the Emperor Hadrian. I also love dear St. Agatha, who was martyred for refusing the "solicitations" of a Roman Senator.

Character Strengths: I am prudent, patient, charitable, forgiving, understanding, joyful, loyal, and industrious.

Character Weaknesses: One time I used the name of the Lord in vain. Another time I committed a sin of envy because Regina Fitzgerald O'Shaughnessy Kiernan got to crown the statue of the Blessed Virgin. I only got to carry the lillies of the valley.

Fun for Nuns

Does Sister ever have any fun? You bet! Sister is very happy when June starts bustin' out all over. She puts all the scissors in a shoe box, all the construction paper on a shelf, and all the Lavatory Passes in her locked desk drawer. Then she has a whole summer for Personal Enrichment. These are some of the things Sister likes to do:

- Go to the Motherhouse and visit elderly Sisters in the Infirmary

- Play volleyball or croquet with other Sisters

- Cut the cancelled stamps off a year's worth of envelopes and send them to the Missions

- Cut pictures out of old magazines to use in decorating the bulletin board for "Our Friends, the Birds" science unit or "People Of Other Lands" social studies unit

- Go to summer school for six weeks to learn The Dewey Decimal System, The ABC's of Adolescent Psychology, Crafts From Ordinary Scraps, or Today's Music: Is It Sinful?

- Go to confession

- Go on a nature hike to learn about insects and morels

- Go to her parent's cottage in the woods and wear PEDAL PUSHERS!

- Find a Walt Disney retrospective and catch all the Saturday matinees

- Send away for a Mother Teresa poster

- Read **The Life of St. Dymphna, Patron of the Mentally Deranged**

A Pair O' Nuns
Or Which Nun has the Dentist's Appointment and Which Nun is the Companion?

Throughout history, nuns always traveled in pairs. You never saw just one nun by herself standing at the bus stop. This Buddy Nun System insured that elderly nuns would find their way back to the convent, and it provided a partner for a game of checkers on long train trips. If a companion got assigned to a nun she didn't like, she would offer it up for the Poor Souls in Purgatory and consider it an opportunity to strengthen her patience, charity, and fortitude. Legend has it that nuns traveled in teams of two for protection. The real reason, known only to Mother Superior, was that it was easier for one nun to run away.

A TV Fantasy: If Sister Ruled the Airwaves

7:00 (3) CREEPING SECULARISM — Mini series. In tonight's episode, elderly, eccentric Sister Sepulchra finds a vial of cheap perfume in the new novice's dresser drawer. Will she pour the contents in the toilet or report the incident to Mother Most Merciful, knowing Mother's history of gouty arthritis? Tension mounts as a long distance call is placed to Rome, where the Holy Father weeps as he attempts to thread a needle. Sister Sepulchra: Lana Santyana. Mother Most Merciful: Wilma Cathode. Perfume: Eau de Sacrilege. (2 hrs. 18 min.) Continued Monday, Tuesday, Wednesday, Thursday, and Friday nights.

7:15 (7) PHONICS FOR THE PHAMILY — Comedy. Jimmy learns about consonant blends and writes a prize-winning essay on "Our Friends, the Adverbs." Later he has a terrible nightmare in which he is attacked by Gerunds, Dangling Modifiers, Split Infinitives, and Predicate Objects who gobble up his Spelling Workbook. Jimmy wakes up half crazed, but joins Sister Grammaria in a hilarious tap sequence, "Please Pass the Parts of Speech." Jimmy: Lance Wombat. Sister Grammaria: Phoebe Avant-Garde. Gerunds, Dangling Modifiers, Split Infinitives and Predicate Objects: members of the Oxford Unabridged Corps de Ballet. (86 min.)

7:30 (9) LENTILS FOR LENT — Sister Mary Moulinex shares her favorite meatless recipes, including Penitential Pie, salmon balls, lima bean and lentil surprise, spinach-stuffed flounder, and bread pudding. (About 15-20 min.)

8:00 (2) CONVENT CAPERS — Mystery. On a dark and stormy night, a mysterious stranger wearing a trench coat and a wide-brimmed hat appears at the Convent of Self-Mortification. He is selling indulgences and boxed All Occasion greeting cards. Sister Tormentia recognizes the stranger as none other than Royce Grimaldi, a boy she laughed at in high school. Will he divulge the nasty secret she has concealed for so many years? Should she buy a box of cards? Sister Tormentia: Dabney Yenbad. Royce Grimaldi: Rick Mal de mer. (4 hrs. 10 min.)

8:30 (4) HABITS THROUGHOUT HISTORY — Documentary. From the garment district in Manhattan to the village seamstresses in Austria and Bosnia-Herzegovina, the construction of the habit is traced from the 12th century. Why BVM's look like little television sets; why Sisters of St. Vincent are called "God's Geese." Sponsored by Acme Starch Company.

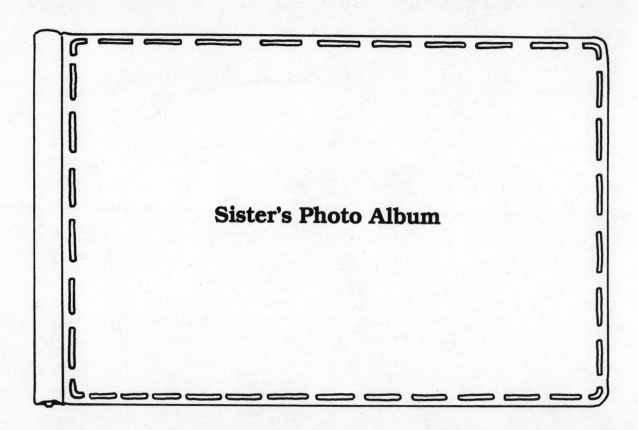

Sister's Photo Album

My beloved parents, Catherine and Joseph. They taught me my morning and evening prayers, made a Marriage Encounter every year, and their children were like vines around their table. Mother was President of the Sanctuary Society at St. Hyacinth's Parish and Dad was the Grand Knight of the Knights of Columbus.

My beloved brothers. Left to right: Matthew, Mark, Luke, and John. Matthew became a Maryknoll Missionary; Mark joined the Jesuits; Luke is a bachelor and lives in Whiting, Indiana; John and his wife have 13 children.

My beloved sisters. Left to right: Mary Catherine, Mary Martha, Mary Margaret, and Mary Therese. Mary Catherine is a nurse-midwife in Zambia; Mary Martha is a clerk at Woolworth's; Mary Margaret distributes leaflets for the Propagation of the Faith; Mary Therese and her husband have 11 children.

My beloved nieces and nephews at the Family Reunion at Loon Lake, August 1983. Left to right: Peter, Paul, Timothy, John, Stephen, Barnabas, Simon, Matthew, Martin, Philip, Thomas, Clare, Cecilia, Agatha, Rose, Elizabeth, Perpetua, Vincent, Agnes, Christopher, Dominic, Francis Xavier, Ignatius, and Cletus.

Mr. Cabrini Sabatini, our beloved Maintenance Man at St. Chrysogonus School. We would be lost without his mop, his bucket, and his industrial size can of sawdust which he sprinkles on the . . . ahem . . . when the children throw up. Mr. Sabatini changes the spark plugs on the convent's Dodge Dart station wagon, replaces broken window glass, and sprays disinfectant in the Boys and Girls bathrooms.

Mr. and Mrs. O'Flaherty. Pillars of the church. Presidents of the Home and School Association, Chairmen of the St. Chrysogonus Fun Fair, Room Parents, Soccer Coaches, Rummage Sale Directors, Bingo Callers, and Chairmen of the St. Patrick's Day Dinner Dance and Fund Raiser. Truly doing God's work on earth!

Mother Most Merciful, our beloved Provincial. Mother gave me $10 from petty cash so I could buy a marble pillar (plastic, really) and a lace runner for the May altar in my classroom. Mother also gave me permission to go home for **two full days** when the bank foreclosed on my parent's mortgage.

Miss Delphine, our beloved organist and music teacher. What would our Corpus Christi Procession be without her? She has recently recorded a number of all-time favorite hymns, including "As Pants the Heart for Jesus."

Sister and Her Students:

S'ter Crazy

THE GRADE SCHOOL NUN: A Moment of Silent Prayer

Oh there are times, dear Lord, I pray
That no one will throw up today;
That Jennifer won't start a fight;
That no one's dog died overnight.

That Sally's party after lunch
Will not include a sweet red punch
Which I will mop up, drip by drip,
While stepping on a chocolate chip.

Timmy's hand is up. I think
He wants to get his nineteenth drink
Or cause a ruckus in the hall
By scribbling swear words on the wall.

I've zipped their jackets, dried their tears,
Taught them numbers, calmed their fears.
I spend each school day nervously
With people under three foot three.

They squirm, they squeak, they wriggle, too;
This classroom is a human zoo.
They lose their crayons, drop their books;
I'd like to hang them all on hooks.

Forgive me if I seem distressed,
But I could use a six month rest.
There are no ifs or ands or buts;
I think I'm slowly going nuts.

If You Were Good, Sister Would Let You . . .

* take the blackboard erasers outside and clap them together to clean them. Girls wearing navy blue uniforms returned to the classroom looking like powdered sugar doughnuts.

* open the door for Father when he came to quiz you about everything in the Baltimore Catechism.

* take the milk money to the Office — a singular honor given only to students of unquestionable integrity.

* control the classroom temperature by using the long, wooden window pole to raise or lower the windows.

* pass the scissors and paste pots for Art Class.

* be the Lunch Line Leader, standing at the front of the ranks as the class filed out (silently and two-by-two).

* deliver a secret message, taped shut, to another Sister's classroom.

* empty the wastebaskets into the smelly, whooshing, frightening school incinerator.

* wash the blackboards and desks as an after-school privilege on Friday afternoons.

* be a Bathroom Monitor, thereby alienating you from your classmates since you felt compelled to snitch if somebody started a water fight, shot spitballs, or used a dirty word.

* add to your burgeoning collection of holy cards by giving you a St. Stephen (being stoned to death) or a St. Elizabeth of Hungary carrying the roses she allegedly found miraculously growing in the snow). Sister always wrote "God Bless You" and signed her name on the back.

If You Were Bad, Sister Would Make You . . .

* move your desk to the front of the room so you could sit RIGHT UNDER HER NOSE — a powerful behavior modification technique accompanied by snickers from the rest of the class.

* diagram 25 extra sentences for homework, all with compound subjects, subordinate clauses, and predicate objects.

* stick your wad of pink bubble gum on the tip of your nose as a visible warning to other miscreants who might be tempted to chew in class.

* write "I Will Not Talk In Line" 100 times (using perfect penmanship), sitting forlornly at your desk while everybody else was on the playground for recess.

* stand in the cloakroom among the snowsuits and galoshes, isolated from polite society

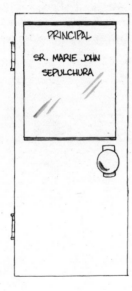

until it was determined that you had seen the error of your ways, repented, and were ready to rejoin the other boys and girls.

* read the note you slipped to Mary Jean OUT LOUD "so the rest of the class can enjoy your little joke."

* take a note home to your parents, telling them how disappointed she was in you, to be returned with their signature by 8:15 the next morning.

* GO TO THE PRINCIPAL'S OFFICE!

The Lunchroom Laws Of Sister Linguine

Praise the Lord, and welcome to Crown of Thorns Lunchroom! Just as our souls need the nourishment of sanctifying grace, our bodies need the nourishment of good, wholesome food so that we may become strong and healthy to do God's work on earth. Please remember these few simple rules so that Sister will not have to remove your tray and send you to the back of the line to start over:

1) Baked beans are not to be referred to as "spit up."

2) Do not blow the paper wrapper off your straw. This is a lunchroom, not an airport.

3) Jesus loves little boys and girls who eat lima beans.

4) Do not roll peas off the edge of the tables.

5) Do not put string beans in your neighbor's apple juice.

6) Be grateful for creamed onions. The starving children in Africa would love to have a nice dish of creamed onions.

7) Do not make disgusting noises when you are told that today's dessert is Prune Jumble.

8) Do not blow through the straw to make bubbles in your chocolate milk that splash on your neighbor's white uniform blouse.

9) God did <u>too</u> invent Brussels sprouts!

10) Do not trade your portion of salmon loaf for another child's brownie. Salmon is a wonderful source of protein.

11) Do not scrape your serving of Prune Jumble into the garbage can. It is a sin to waste food.

12) Please do not whisper to your neighbor, "If it isn't pizza, to hell with it."

13) It is not amusing to smear chocolate pudding on your neighbor's arithmetic homework paper.

How Well Do You Know Your Nuns?

QUESTIONS

Okay, so everybody knows nuns don't have hair, they never sweat, and their idea of fun is a weekend of self-denial. But do you really know your nuns? Here's a fun little quiz for all you Soldiers of Christ out there! (Answers on page   Don't peek!

TRUE   FALSE

1) Sister entered the convent because her boyfriend entered the seminary. _____ _____

2) There's a secret tunnel between the convent and the rectory. _____ _____

3) Sister thinks Bing Crosby really was ordained. _____ _____

4) Sister wishes she didn't have to explain the Sixth Commandment to her Third graders. Or the Ninth. _____ _____

5) Sister likes little girls better than little boys. _____ _____

How Well Do You Know Your Nuns?

ANSWERS

1) False. Sister never had a boyfriend.

2) False. This rumor was started by a disgruntled parent whose son had to repeat second grade two years in a row.

3) False. Sister knows a divorced man cannot be ordained. She's very glad that Barry Fitzgerald made it, though.

4) True. Sister excuses herself from the classroom when it's time for Father to come in for Religion and handle those red hot numbers!

5) True. Sister favors neatness, obedience, promptness, and good behavior. Boys are sweaty, defiant, tardy, and can belch on command.

Aa Bb Cc Dd Ee Ff Gg Hh Ii Jj Kk Ll

The Palmer Method

Sister made you practice seven million ovals during Penmanship class. Your best paper looked like this:

llllllllllllllllllllllllll
llllllllllllllllllllllllll

and so forth.

You also had to practice capital M's seven million times. Like this:

mmmmmmmmmmmmmmmmmmm
mmmmmmmmmmmmmmmmmmm

Aa Bb Cc Dd Ee Ff Gg Hh Ii Jj Kk Ll

Aa Bb Cc Dd Ee Ff Gg
Hh Ii Jj Kk Ll Mm
Nn Oo Pp Qq Rr Ss Tt
Uu Vv Ww Xx Yy Zz

For Christmas, Sister
made you give your parents
a Spiritual Bouquet. You
promised them

	25	Masses
	25	Holy Communions
	25	Rosaries
	1,689	Ejaculations

At age 43 you still feel

Aa Bb Cc Dd Ee Ff Gg Hh Ii Jj Kk Ll

tremendous guilt because
you never did finish
all that stuff.

On every paper, you
had to put your name
and the date in the
upper right-hand corner.
In the middle, you had
to put
J. M. J.

That stood for "Jesus,
Mary, and Joseph" who

Aa Bb Cc Dd Ee Ff Gg Hh Ii Jj Kk Ll

also liked perfect penmanship.

 So how come, now that
you're grown up, nobody
can read your handwriting?

Youth Wants To Know

QUESTIONS GUARANTEED TO WILT A WIMPLE

1. If God is all-good, why does He let planes crash?

2. If God is all-wise, does He understand fiber optics?

3. If God is all-kind, why did my hamster die?

4. If free will is so great, why did Eve eat the apple?

5. How do babies get out of Limbo?

6. What does my soul look like?

7. Is Michael Jackson a near occasion of sin?

8. How long is eternity?

9. Why did God invent spiders?

10. Did you ever say a swear?

11. Can you fly like Sally Field?

12. Can I go to the bathroom?

Tips For Catholic Parents

Moms! Dads! Is your daughter closing the door on Jesus? Or is there a vocation hidden under that Esprit sweatshirt? Does she have The Calling? Can you help her choose to be a Bride of Christ?

Start her on the path to perfection by giving her the RIGHT name! Not Dawn, Heather, Tamara, or Buffie — instead, choose one of the following convent-approved names:

Theresa	Anne	Margaret
Monica	Agatha	Bridget
Elizabeth	Martha	Frances
Catherine	Judith	Bernadette

Put a "Mary" in front, and she's guaranteed all A's in grade school!

You might want to consider changing the family name, too, unless it's been mentioned in a Bing Crosby movie:

Dwyer	Sweeney	Dugan
Fitzgerald	Kelly	Sullivan
McGinty	Finnegan	O'Toole
Haggerty	Cannon	McCormick

Music Class

Music class was a simple way to kill a Friday afternoon, when everybody was staring at the clock (right between the portraits of George Washington and the Sacred Heart) and counting the minutes until the dismissal bell rang. Friday afternoon was no time to tackle long division or dangling participles, so Sister Mary St. Cecilia would "come in" for Music Class.

Early in the school year, Sister divided the class into four groups: Robins, Bluebirds, Grackles, and Crows. She thought you couldn't figure out that if you were a Crow, it was all over for you at Carnegie Hall.

Robins and Bluebirds were always girls. They memorized all the words, and they could all carry a tune. Boys fidgeted, cleaned their fingernails, slipped <u>Archie and Veronica</u> comics into their music books, and burped on command to drive Sister crazy.

Before you could actually sing a song, you had to clap quarter notes. Then eighth notes. Then sixteenth notes. Third grade ended up sounding like a standing ovation for Mitch Miller and The Gang.

There were songs for Hallowe'en, songs for Thanksgiving, songs for Easter, songs for Welcoming the Springtime. But each month had a special hymn, often in the key of C and 4/4 time . . .

Song of the Month

September Song

Leading off the school year in September, the class learned "Come, Holy Ghost." After all, He was the font of wisdom (not many eight year olds knew what a font was, but it sounded OK), and wisdom sounded like a good thing to have.

> Come, Holy Ghost, Creator blest,
> And in our hearts take up Thy rest.
> Come with Thy grace, and heav'nly aid
> To fill the hearts which Thou hast made;
> To fill the hearts which Thou hast made.

The Falling Leaves . . .

October was The Month of The Holy Rosary, and Sister always made a gigantic, larger-than-life-sized Rosary out of colored construction paper and pasted it to the blackboard behind her desk. Anybody who could correctly recite the Joyful, Sorrowful, and Glorious Mysteries got a "Blessed Mother Loves You" holy card. During Music Class, we sang:

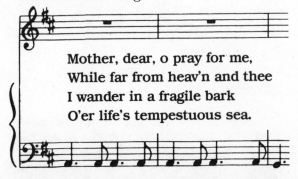

> Mother, dear, o pray for me,
> While far from heav'n and thee
> I wander in a fragile bark
> O'er life's tempestuous sea.

The North Wind Doth Blow

By now the class repertoire was growing fast. November was notable because it started off on the 1st with All Saints' Day, followed immediately on the 2nd by All Souls' Day, which was set aside to honor those poor unfortunate people who died with a little smidgen of sin on their souls and were in a holding pattern in Limbo until somebody prayed them out of there and on up to heaven. There were no hymns in their honor, however.

Because there were about 62 zillion saints, we couldn't work all their names into one hymn (after all, what rhymes with Hippolytus or Sylvester or Frances Xavier Cabrini?) so we simply sang:

> To all the Saints who from their labors rest
> Who Thee by faith before the world confess;
> Thy name, O Jesus, be forever blest;
> Al-le-lu-ia . . . Al-le-lu-ia!

I'm A Little Snowflake . . .

December was easy. Once in awhile Sister would let us sing "Rudolph, the Red Nosed Reindeer," but usually that was the theme of our heathen brethren in public schools who were being taught by infidels and didn't know any better. We were big on Wise Men, the Star in the East, an assortment of shepherds, and Wind Through the Olive Trees (Softly Did Blow, "Round Little Bethlehem, Long, Long Ago). In our piping sopranos, we sang:

> O light of all the world,
> O wond'rous Babe Divine;
> Send out Thy grace to light our hearts
> And make us truly Thine.

The Feast Of The What?

After Christmas vacation, January was a real bummer. The Holy Day of Obligation that fell on January 1st commemorated the Circumcision of Our Lord. Nobody ever wrote a hymn about that. Even Sister didn't talk about it very much.

My Funny St. Valentine

Valentine's Day provided one of the few occasions for levity during the dreary, endless Lenten Season. Sister spent several Recreation Periods in the Convent at night making a "mail box" out of a packing carton. She'd cut a slit in the top and paste red hearts and white doilies on the sides. The mail box sat on a special table in the corner at the front of the room until February 14th when Mary Catherine, notorious Teacher's Pet, was allowed to be the Mailman and pass out the Valentines that had been stuffed into the box.

Sister reminded us that this secular feast, in truth, honored Saint Valentine, a holy Roman priest who ministered to a great number of martyrs during the persecution of Claudius II. Like so many saints, Valentine himself was martyred during the reign of Aurelian in 270 AD.

In keeping with the spirit of hearts and flowers, we sang:

 To Jesus' heart all-burning
With fervent love for men
My heart with fondest yearning
Shall raise the joyful strain.
While ages course along,
Blest be with loudest song
The Sacred Heart of Jesus
On ev'ry heart and tongue;
The Sacred Heart of Jesus
On ev'ry heart and tongue.

Mary Catherine always got the most Valentines. Big Billy Magruder, The Dumbest Kid in Class, only got one, and everybody knew he'd sent it to himself.

Mary Catherine's mother baked cupcakes with pink frosting and put a candy heart on top of each one. Big Billy Magruder got the heart that said "Get Lost." The one on Sister's cupcake said "Hey Babe."

March-ing Along Together:

St. Patrick and St. Joseph

On March 17th all the Irish kids wore green sweaters or hair ribbons, and even Sister — whose name from home was Czerwinski — pinned a shamrock to her habit. If you were Lithuanian or German or Italian, you had to pretend your name was O'Krivstcz or O'Montevelli.

Sister plopped on the piano bench to head a rounding rendition of Hail, Glorious St. Patrick:

Hail, glorious St. Patrick, dear saint of our Isle!

To us thy poor children be gracious the while,

We pray to thee high in the mansions above,

On Erin's green valleys to look down in love.

In the war against sin, in the fight for the faith,

Dear saint may thy children resist to the death.

Their strength be in meekness, in penance, and prayer;

Their banner the cross which they glory to bear.

March 19th was the second part of the double header, the day set aside to honor St. Joseph — no less than the Patron of the Universal Church and one heck of a carpenter to boot.

> **Dear Saint Joseph pure and gentle,**
> **Guardian of the Savior Child;**
> **Treading with the Virgin Mother**
> **Egypt's deserts rough and wild.**
> **Hail St. Joseph, Spouse of Mary,**
> **Bless'd above all saints on high;**
> **When the death shades round us gather,**
> **Teach us, teach us how to die.**

This got you revved up to enjoy the rest of the Lenten Season when you gave up candy, movies, ice skating, and everything else in life that was enjoyable. By April 1st you'd have killed for a box of Milk Duds.

April Agonies

Before you could tear into your Easter basket and gobble up the chocolate marshmallow bunnies, you had to live through Holy Week which featured one dreary procession after another. The Church was dark and cold, the statues covered with purple shrouds, and no organ playing was allowed.

Instead, Sister blew her pitch pipe to lead the children in the mournful Latin hymn, "Stabat Mater Dolorosa":

> **Stabat Mater Dolorosa**
> **Juxta crucem lacrimosa**
> **Dum pendebat Filius.**
> Or,
> **By the Cross her station keeping,**

Stood the mournful Mother weeping,
Close to Jesus to the last.

It all paid off by Easter Sunday, when the organ rang out once more and Sister led the class in that golden oldie:

The dawn was purpl'ing o'er the sky
With Alleluias rang the air;
This earth held glor'ious jubilee
Hell gnashed its teeth in fierce despair.

'Tis The Month Of Our Mother

Mary Catherine always got to crown the statue of the Blessed Virgin, and Sister encouraged the students to bring bouquets of lillies-of-the-valley, tulips, daffodils, and what-ever other spring flowers they could snip from Ma's garden. The May Altar was set up on the table in the front of the room; the blue and white statue of Mary stood in front of a blue and white corrugated paper shrine. Every Blessed Virgin statue showed Mary with her right foot on the head of a snake, single-footedly crushing out evil, sin, and bad behavior in the entire world.

May's Hit Parade was a musical feast; there were probably more hymns written to, for, and about Mary than any other Catholic superstar.

The highlight happened when Mary Catherine lifted the crown of spring flowers and placed it on the statue's head. Our big number was:

'Tis the month of Our Mother,
The blessed and beautiful days;
When our lips and our spirits
Are glowing with love and with praise.

The Times, They Are A-Changin'

After centuries of singing about crowns of thorns, martyrs who had their tongues cut out, and hearts o'ercome with the guilt of mortal sin, Catholics changed their tune. They embraced major chords and filled their hymnals with songs about the spirit blowin' from the mountaintop. Led by the Music Nun, the "guitar Mass" became a regular feature of the weekend liturgy. Several devout adolescents gathered INSIDE THE ALTAR RAIL with their Gibson guitars to strum a lot of Meaningful Music. Despite Sister's pitch pipe, the instruments were never exactly tuned and as a result, one young strummer's G was another young strummer's G$^{\#}$.

Not to worry. The spirit was upon them, and Sister was leading them in a thin, reedy voice. Older parishoners continued to read the Mass in Latin while the pre-pubescents twanged away, often in a style that blended The New Christy Minstrels with Sha Na Na.

Parishes throughout the nation reverberated to the African beat of the hymn at the top of the charts — "Kumbaya." Musical historians differ as to the origin of this incredibly dull song; some say it was brought to this country by The Shondelles after a successful concert tour in Rwanda and Zimbabwe. Others claim that its source is a tribal phrase meaning either "may your manioc be cooked" or "peace be to your wildebeest."

Whatever, "Kumbaya" had two things in its favor: Sister only had to teach three chords, and the song calls upon Our Lord four times in each verse. Pastors, given to simple pleasures, liked that.

Kumbaya

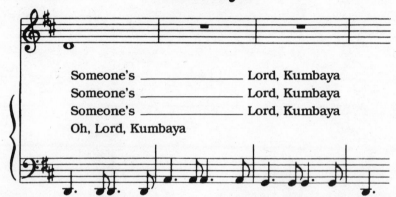

Someone's _____ Lord, Kumbaya
Someone's _____ Lord, Kumbaya
Someone's _____ Lord, Kumbaya
Oh, Lord, Kumbaya

Fill in the blanks with any of the following:

Praying, singing, napping, living, fainting, loving, crying, sneezing, dying, teaching, hoping, whining, scratching, trying, learning, dusting, eating, wishing, talking, driving, swimming, flying, stooping, knitting, chanting, climbing, shouting, screaming, spelling, ironing, bowling, shopping, showering, skateboarding, whistling, laying linoleum, sniveling, attending graduate school, leaving on a jet plane, playing ice hockey, having gall stones removed, cleaning the silver, putting up aluminum siding, taking a civil service exam, clipping nose hairs, straining pasta shells, defrosting the fridge, making yogurt, breaking wind, twisting coat hangers into weird shapes, smearing themselves with guacamole dip, kiting checks, calling toll free, etc., etc., etc.,

Graduation Day

Having completed eight years of "Yesster," "Noster," and "I'm sorry, Ster," the graduating class files into church on a muggy June night to receive their diplomas from the pastor. During his homily, Father cautions them that "this is not an end, but a beginning," and thunderously reminds them of the endless, major sacrifices made on their behalf by the Good Sisters, by their Devoted Parents, by the members of their Loving Families. He urges them to strive for personal holiness in a secular world by saying "Yes" to Christ and "No" to Satan. He prays that they will never forget the valuable lessons they learned during their years at Blazing Martyrs Parochial School.

Sister Melodica revs up the mighty pipe organ in the choir loft and plays the opening bars of the school anthem:

"Farewell, dear Blazing Martyrs,
To thee we shall be true;
We'll ne'er forget your colors —
Eternal black and blue."

The girls sniffle — partly out of sentiment and partly because their feet are killing them in their white satin heels — while the boys, whose voices are changing, stare at their fingernails and mouth the words lest they croak in the wrong spot.

Young Catholic males are channeled into the masculine world of St. George and the Dragon Academy and, except for the occasional "Girl's Bid" dance in the gym at Daughters of Denial High, they are free of daily scrutiny by the sharp eyes of the nuns. They confront another force in Catholic education . . . the Jesuit. But that is another book.

Young Catholic females, of course, are destined for four more years of "Yesster," "Noster," and "I'm sorry, Ster" in the rarified atmosphere of the all girls' high school. In addition to a rigorous academic program, the girls are encouraged to participate in varsity swimming, debate, arts and crafts, foods and nutrition, volleyball, newspaper and yearbook, Dads and Daughters Dance committee, Lenten Liturgy committee, glee club, drama club, personal prayer study groups, swing band, creative crocheting, and the pompon squad.

The nuns are convinced that all of this frenetic activity will keep the girls' bodies on the brink of exhaustion and their minds off of . . . BOYS! The strategy is not totally successful, since most adolescent girls would kill for reliable information about adolescent boys, no matter how tired they are. There is something vaguely unsatisfying about having girls play male roles in the Senior Class presentation of "Hamlet." Sister Theatricus is a Shakespearean scholar who chose this particular play because of its one memorable line: "GET THEE TO A NUNNERY!"

Sister Theatricus is only one of several Vocation Spotters scattered throughout the faculty. Vocation Spotters are known to approach from the rear, quietly, and tap a student on the shoulder while whispering, "Mary Jeanne, have you considered that you might have The Calling?" Other Vocation Spotters suggest a weekend at the Motherhouse, a Day of Recollection at a local retreat house, or searching the inner self to open one's ears to the noble summons.

Sister Devotionella taught Social Sciences, Personal Hygiene, and Beginning Theology. A member of the order for 47 years, she had several hundred True Vocations to her credit. Sister kept a small statue of the Virgin Mary on a corner of her desk; the girls noticed that the statue faced a different part of the classroom each Monday morning. The mystery remained unsolved until the last week of school, when Sister confessed that she had been pointing the statue at different girls each week in the hope that the Blessed Mother would help them discover within themselves a true and lasting vocation to the convent.

Sister was responsible for teaching the girls something called "You and Your Body," which emphasized personal hygiene and cleanliness — which, of course, is next to Godliness. This topic can become a sensitive one, particularly for adolescent girls who are forced to wear the same navy blue serge uniform every day during an entire academic year. In the era before wash 'n wear, the uniform visited the dry cleaners only twice in ten months: during Christmas and Easter vacations. Scientific advances in underarm deodorants couldn't compete with terminal perspiration, particularly in the early fall and spring when the classrooms were broiling hot and Sister refused to open the windows lest a confused insect fly into the room and terrorize the student population.

The fifteenth, and final, lesson plan covering "You and Your Body" had to do with — well, reproduction in mammals. Sister was grateful for filmstrips supplied by the American Farm Bureau which featured basic biological functions performed by mammals both large and small. The final lesson was illustrated with blurry photographs on the screen showing the diagram of a pregnant cow. Sister explained that the mother cow obviously had a baby cow inside her. Sister asked if there were any questions.

Of course there were. Hundreds of them. Like, "how is that thing going to get out of there?" or, more to the point, "how did it get in there?" Some girls even wondered, silently, what relevance the pregnant cow had in their own lives.

The girls, of course, were too embarrassed to ask questions. Sister would have been too embarrassed to answer them. So the girls entered the mysterious world of dating, marriage, and motherhood with a pitiful lack of information and were secretly delighted to find a much more complete explanation in "All Creatures Great and Small."

Many of the girls, however, chose to enter the convent after completing this course, believing that marriage and motherhood were somehow directly related to successful dairy farming.

The
Seven Stages
of
Sisterhood:

From Here to Eternity

- Infancy
- Early childhood
- Childhood
- Adolescence
- Young Adulthood
- The Middle Years
- Readin', Rockin', Retired

Infancy

IT'S A GIRL! Soon after her birth, Mary Angelica's parents realized that there was something different about their baby daughter. While most infants reeked of stale formula and fossilized rice cereal, Mary Angelica remained sweet-smelling and fragrant . . . could it be . . . the odor of sanctity! Observing their deep-seated religious traditions, they pinned a Miraculous Medal to the baby's diapers to ward off the Powers of Darkness while she napped. At her Baptismal Rite, instead of spitting the salt off her tongue and shrieking as most infants do, Mary Angelica smiled, ate the salt, and made the Sign of the Cross with her tiny fist. Her favorite teething aid was an oversized, gaily colored wooden rosary; for six months she gnawed through the Joyful, Sorrowful, and Glorious Mysteries. Her grandmothers on both sides embroidered a set of liturgical bibs for each day of the year, and there were often strained prunes covering the words "This is the Third Sunday of Advent" or "Blessed Are Those Who Hunger, For They Shall Have Their Fill." Mary Angelica's first words were not "Mama" or "Dada," but "I want to be Confirmed."

Early Childhood

Mary Angelica kept the points very sharp on all her 64 crayons, and sat quietly coloring for hours. She always stayed inside the lines. Her favorite coloring books were "Let's Go to Vatican City" and "Fun With The Old Testament." While other children were wallowing in the dirt and making mud pies, Mary Angelica was making starch so she could use her Little Homemaker iron on the habit of her Missionary Sister doll. Instead of asking the usual childhood questions, such as "Where do babies come from?" Mary Angelica would ask, "Mama, what's a Plenary Indulgence?" When her eight year old brother put a dead mouse in her doll house kitchen, she did not punch his lights out. No. She said, "I'll pray for you, Timmy." Mary Angelica loved to play dress up at Grandma's house. She'd slip her little feet into black oxfords, pin a white handkerchief on her head, wrap herself in a brown chenille bedspread, hang Grandma's

rosary around her neck, and annouce, "Me a Dominican." Her musical talent surfaced at an early age, and she delighted the family for hours on end singing "Jesus Wants Me for a Sunbeam" and "'Tis the Month of Our Mother."

Childhood

As soon as she learned to tell time, Mary Angelica awakened her parents at 5:45 every Sunday morning so they wouldn't be late for the 10:00 Children's Mass. She often stayed after school — not because she was naughty, but because she loved to wash paste off the desks and help Sister alphabetize the holy cards. She thought boys were yukky. Boys thought she was yukky. They bombarded her with spitballs when she was appointed Room Monitor to keep order in the class while Sister stepped out for a few moments on some mysterious errand. (To go to the bathroom? Perish the thought!) Mary Angelica recorded their names, reported them to Sister, and smiled smugly when they were ordered to "March yourselves right to the Pincipal's Office!" She donated her weekly allowance, plus a small inheritance from her grandfather, to the Holy Childhood Association for the purpose of ransoming pagan babies. By

the time she finished seventh grade there were 5,392 Southeast Asians and several hundred Africans all named Mary Angelica. During graduation ceremonies, her parents fought back tears of pride as she was awarded the medal for Perfect Attendance All Eight Years.

Adolescence

Mary Angelica did not spend Saturday night with her friends at the roller skating rink. She chose to make weekend retreats instead, where she read the next several chapters of The Catholic Girl's Guide and, after nine hours of Private Examination of Conscience, discovered several character flaws that needed to be conquered on her road to Personal Sanctity. She spent Tuesday evenings at Mother of Perpetual Help Devotions, and liked nothing better than being first in line for Confessions on Saturday afternoon. She hung around the convent a lot, running small errands for the nuns to buy a book of postage stamps or a large bottle of aspirin. Her handwriting was almost perfect by now. She spent her summers at Villa Sanctissimus, where she learned to sing 15th Century plain chant and to tat the lace trim for several hundred altar cloths. She saved stamps for the Missions, and prayed for the Conversion of

Russia. It became clear to Mary Angelica's parents that they were not losing a daughter . . . they were gaining a Postulant!

Young Adulthood

It was the happiest day of her life — well, maybe tied for first place with the day she received her First Holy Communion. Mary Angelica took the veil! She entered the polished, scrubbed, waxed, quiet, orderly, disciplined world of the Handmaidens of Endless Atonement. She learned to make May altars out of marble pillars and white corrugated paper. She looked forward to the pancake supper on Shrove Tuesday, the last occasion for levity before the forty dready days of Lent. Sister Mary Sassafrass, the convent cook, placed twenty well-scrubbed and sterilized dimes in the pancake batter, and whoever found a dime in her pancake . . . got to keep it! Mary Angelica got to go home on Christmas Day — with her companion, of course — but had to be back at the convent by 5 p.m. or dark, whichever came first. Because they returned at 5:07 p.m., Mary Angelica and her companion had to write a "Dark Letter" to Sister Provincial, explaining

their tardiness and begging forgiveness. Next year, Mary Angelica would caution her mother to start the turkey roasting at 8 a.m. instead of 9.

The Middle Years

Mary Angelica had taught second grade for 34 years in a row. She did not understand why second graders chewed the erasers off of lead pencils and then jammed the erasers into their ears. She did not understand why second graders threw up more than any other age group in the entire school. She did not understand why, in addition to teaching second grade, she had to organize the Crossing Cadets, the Girls' Bathroom Monitors, the Bingo Concessions, the Boy Jesus Club, the Cherubim Choraliers, the Archdiocesan Spelldown, and the Altar Boys' League. Rocco Cavelli was an altar boy. When the Bishop agreed to celebrate a Pontifical High Mass one Easter Sunday, Rocco Cavelli slipped into the sanctuary and unscrewed the four brass bells that were rung at the most solemn part of the Mass. When Marty McHanrahan, Rocco's partner, picked up the bells to ring them, they clanged and clattered and made a horrendous racket as they bounced down the altar steps. Mary Angelica has never stopped praying for Rocco Cavelli. Mary Angelica wonders if Monther Provincial would grant her request for a year's sabbatical.

Readin', Rockin', Retired

Mildly arthritic, Mary Angelica began her well-earned retirement at the Motherhouse of the Handmaidens of Endless Atonement. Set high on a bluff overlooking the Mississippi River, Mount Atonement was home to the elderly nuns who had spent a lifetime teaching reading, writing, and arithmetic. Mary Angelica corresponded with many of her former students — except Rocco Cavelli — and completed the construction of several hundred rosaries. She enjoyed watching reruns of "Leave It To Beaver," "Wild Kingdom," and "Father Knows Best." Mary Angelica retained the full habit, even though the order had approved secular dress in 1966. She never fully understood how women could wear trousers, especially her fellow Sisters. She said her Daily Office, prayed for the deceased members of her family and the Poor Souls in Purgatory. On her 89th birthday she completed all the Spiritual Bouquets she had

promised people when she was in fourth grade. Now, at last, she could go home to Heaven.

Are You Closing The Door On Jesus?
Or Do You Have a True Vocation?

Test Yourself! Test Yourself!

Stuck in a dead-end job? Tired of dumping frozen french fries into endless vats of hot grease? Sick of scooping double-dip Rocky Road sugar cones? Maybe it's time for a change! The following quiz, prepared by the author in conjunction with leading psychologists, theologians, and biorhythm specialists, will help you determine if you might be a candidate for the fast-paced and challenging career of a Roman Catholic nun.

Put your name and today's date in the upper right hand corner. Answer A, B, or C.

1. Which of the following career choices appeal most to you?

    A) Cocktail waitress, actress, "21" dealer in Vegas.

    B) Avon Lady, Tupperware District Manager, hair designer.

    C) Librarian, organist, missionary.

2. As a youngster, you liked to:

    A) Throw dead beetles at your little brother.

    B) Play with Dionne Quintuplets paper dolls.

    C) Pretend you were St. Joan of Arc.

3. Your favorite birthday present was:

   A) A Swiss Army Knife.

   B) A Smurf sticker book.

   C) A rosary that was blessed by the Pope.

4. Choose the outfit you'd love to wear:

   A) Black beret, white plastic triangle earrings, see-through blouse with black bra, pink skirt, 6" wide green vinyl belt, black net stockings with seams, pink ballet slippers.

   B) Levi's, Notre Dame sweatshirt, lavender running shoes.

   C) Calf length polyester skirt, brown sweater, brown orthopedic oxfords.

5. Your bedroom is decorated with posters of:

   A) Iron Maiden and Judas Priest.

   B) Buddy Holly and James Dean.

   C) Pope John Paul II and Perry Como.

6. Your favorite movie is:

   A) Madonna's "A Certain Sacrifice."

   B) "Gone With the Wind"

   C) "The Song of Bernadette"

7. The following hairstyle is The Real You:

   A) Mohawk with streaks of purple, green, and pink.

   B) Wavy perm, lots of mousse.

   C) Bun.

8. As a young girl, you thought your parents:

   A) Must have been born in the 17th century.

   B) Had a lot of fun in the Couples' Bridge Marathon.

   C) Were infallible.

9. The "Man of Your Dreams":

   A) Drives a Harley Hog, has a pierced ear, drinks gin on the rocks, raises pit bulls.

   B) Uses Brut, likes soap-on-a-rope, wears Ralph Lauren chinos, drives a BMW 320i.

   C) Drives a 1977 Chevy Nova, wears black wing-tips, sells aluminum awnings, lives with his 76-year-old mother.

10. The very best book you ever read was:

    A) **The Life and Times of The Marquis de Sade.**

    B) **Crossings**, by Danielle Steel.

    C) **The Bobbsey Twins at the Seashore**, by Laura Lee Hope.

11. Your favorite magazine is:

    A) **Cycle World.**

    B) **Cosmopolitan.**

    C) **Reader's Digest.**

How to Determine Your Score

Give yourself one point for each "A" answer, two for each "B," and three for each "C." If you scored from 7 to 11 points, forget it. You're not closing the door on Jesus; you'll never even hear him ring the bell.

If you scored 11 to 15 points, you might want to examine your conscience and make a weekend Retreat to decide whether convent life is your cup of tea. You can always cancel the subscription to **Cosmopolitan**.

If you scored higher than 15 points, Jesus is whispering in your ear. Think of how proud your parents would be to have a nun in the family! Think of the fun you'd have singing second soprano in the convent choir! Think of the reward you'll earn in Heaven through a lifetime of self-denial, penance, chastity, silent prayer, and personal mortification!

Go ahead — open the door to Jesus. Take a little time right now to fill out the application on page 78

The

END

Unless . . .

Application to the Postulancy
Sorrowful Sisters of St. Symphorosa

Name: _____

Address _____

Grade School _____

High School _____

Height _____ Weight _____ Birth Date _____

Hobbies _____

_____

_____

_____

Why Do You Want To Become A Sorrowful Sister: _____

_____

_____

_____

_____

Who Are Your Favorite Saints: _____

_____

_____

_____

_____

Character Strengths: _____

_____

_____

Character Weaknesses: _____

_____

_____

_____